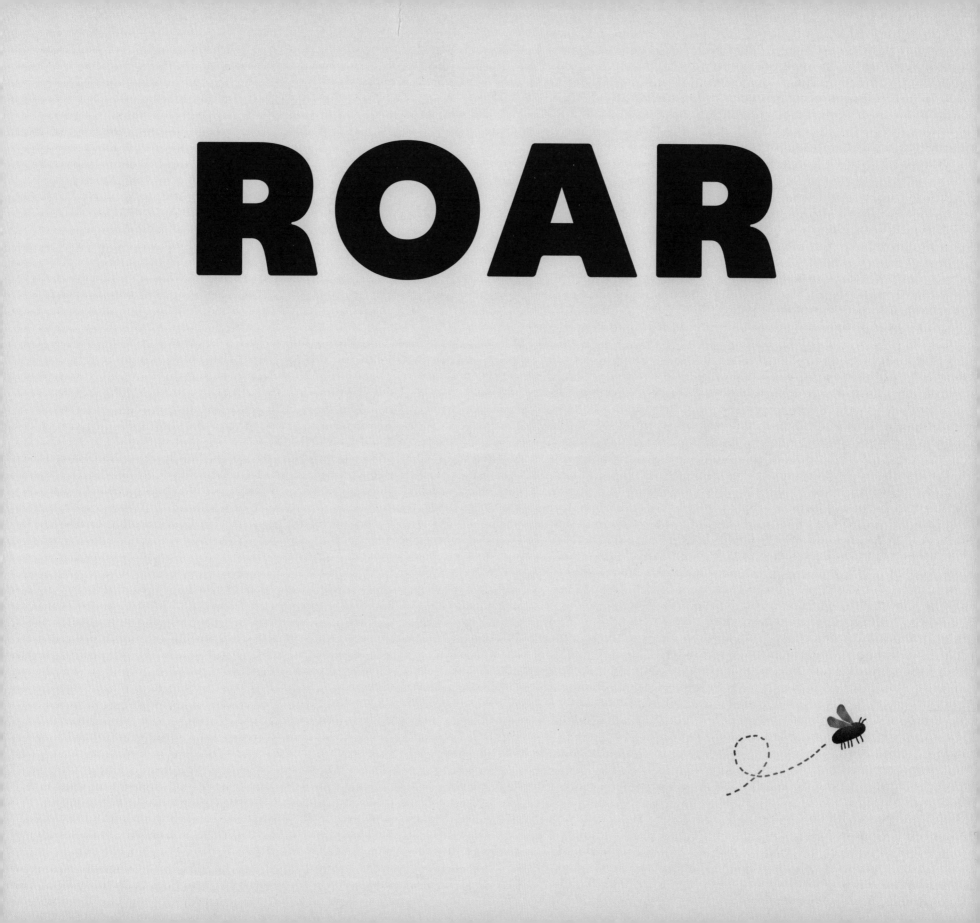

ROAR

A great big thank you to . . .
Alison, Christine, Emma, Mary, Meryl,
Stephanie, and Strawberrie for all the support
and trust bringing this book to life!

BLOOMSBURY CHILDREN'S BOOKS
Bloomsbury Publishing Inc., part of Bloomsbury Publishing Plc
1385 Broadway, New York, NY 10018

BLOOMSBURY, BLOOMSBURY CHILDREN'S BOOKS, and the Diana logo
are trademarks of Bloomsbury Publishing Plc

First published in Great Britain in October 2020 by Bloomsbury Publishing Plc
Published in the United States of America in June 2021
by Bloomsbury Children's Books

Bloomsbury books may be purchased for business or promotional use. For information on
bulk purchases please contact Macmillan Corporate and Premium Sales Department at
specialmarkets@macmillan.com

Library of Congress Cataloging-in-Publication Data
Names: Kerouli, Katerina, author, illustrator. l Kerouli, Katerina, illustrator.
Title: Roar : a book of animal sounds / by Katerina Kerouli ; illustrated by Katerina Kerouli.
Description: New York : Bloomsbury Children's Books, 2021.
Summary: Illustrations and simple, rhyming text invite the reader on a jungle adventure to seek Tiger,
Crocodile, Monkey, and other animals, lifting flaps to reveal the sound each makes.
Identifiers: LCCN 2020050075
ISBN 978-1-5476-0641-2 (hardcover)
Subjects: LCSH: Lift-the-flap books—Specimens. l CYAC: Stories in rhyme. l Jungle animals—Fiction. l
Animal sounds—Fiction. l Lift-the-flap books. l Toy and movable books.
Classification: LCC PZ8.3.K3993 Ro 2021 l DDC [E]—dc23
LC record available at https://lccn.loc.gov/2020050075

Typeset in Futura
Book design by Strawberrie Donnelly
Printed in China by Leo Paper Products, Heshan, Guangdong
2 4 6 8 10 9 7 5 3 1

All papers used by Bloomsbury Publishing Plc are natural, recyclable products made from wood grown in well-managed forests.
The manufacturing processes conform to the environmental regulations of the country of origin.

To find out more about our authors and books visit www.bloomsbury.com and sign up for our newsletters.

ROAR

Katerina Kerouli

BLOOMSBURY
CHILDREN'S BOOKS

NEW YORK LONDON OXFORD NEW DELHI SYDNEY

Tiger, Tiger,
is that you,
hiding in
the tall bamboo?

Such stripy stripes,
such sharp,
sharp claws,
such furry ears,
such big
wide jaws!

Crocodile, Crocodile,
do you lurk there,
with your beady
black-eyed stare?

Snake, Snake,
is that you I spy,
slithering and
sliding by?

Such pointy teeth,
your tail so long,
such scaly scales,
and jaws
so strong.

Such colorful scales,
such a flicky tongue,
such pointy fangs . . .
Look out,
everyone!

Monkey, Monkey,
in the tree,
is that your
curly tail I see?

Such soft brown fur,
such a hairy chin,
such sparkling eyes,
such a
cheeky grin.

Lion, Lion,
with your golden mane,
are you on the
prowl again?

King of the jungle,
so strong and proud,
your gaze
so fierce,
your call
so loud.

The end!